HELEN HOUSE

TEXT

Kayla Kumari Upadhyaya

IMAGES

Kira Gondeck-Silvia

BURROW PRESS | ORLANDO, FL

for Alex

First printed in limited edition hardcover, 2022
Text © Kayla Kumari Upadhyaya, pocket edition 2023
Art © Kira Gondeck-Silvia
Book + Cover Design: Ryan Rivas
Published by Burrow Press
ISBN: 978-1-941681-28-2

I don't know if it's the beginning, but this is where I'll start. Two weeks before I met her parents, Amber said she had something important to tell me. Her timing wasn't great. I'd just slipped my tongue in her open mouth, and it sounded like she was speaking into a cave. Damp, swallowed words, her teeth scraping my tongue. It felt good. All I could hear was "important" and "tell you."

"Can it wait?" I asked, pinching off her bra. It fell to the floor, she kissed me, and I thought *that's that*. It was the start of a new semester, and our schedules were mucked up to the point sex had become a weekend-only activity. But on that particular Monday, we found ourselves with a rare pocket of nothing. No work (although, to be fair, there was always work to be done on my dissertation), no plans, nothing. I'd returned home from a jog immensely horny and texted Amber assuming she'd be busy. *I need you*, I typed and then deleted. *I need you in my mouth*, I texted instead. We'd only been together a year, too early for sex to dwindle, but I was putting off raising that concern. I worried what else it might kick up.

We kept kissing, and I opened my eyes, a habit Amber and every girl I've ever been with hates, but what's so wrong with wanting to see someone? I love looking at the ugly, open wound of someone's kissing mouth. From that close, everyone looks the same.

Before I'd ever been kissed with living lips, I kissed every surface I could find—the top of my desk at school (when I was certain no one was looking), the handle of my bedroom door, magazines I stole from my sister's room that smelled like her friends, the fruity scents of their body sprays soured by sweat. Sometimes, I'd perch on top of the bathroom sink and make out with my reflection in the mirror, always with my eyes open, tonguing the cold, hard surface.

I liked to pretend. I learned it from my sister. Late at night when we were supposed to be asleep, I'd sneak into her room so she could tell me ghost stories. It started when we were very young. She had just started reading big-girl chapter books, and I was jealous, always wishing I could fast-forward time, even then, to catch up with her. She had a collection of fairy tales, and she read them over and

over to me. Hansel & Gretel was her favorite. She said we were like the fabled siblings, casting me as the brother, which I didn't mind. But we got sick of the repetition, and one night she started making up stories instead of reading them, a kind gift to soothe my jealousy.

But once more, I was jealous. This time of her gift for storytelling. She was so good at it. The worlds she concocted out of thin air were wondrous and alive, and I tricked myself into believing that maybe I could one day go to them. My sister saw things other people couldn't, otherworlds calling to us.

In my favorite ghost story of hers, I was the protagonist, a ghost who played strange pranks on mean girls from our neighborhood. I loved this spirit version of myself my sister had made. She was, except for being dead, exactly who I wanted to be. Tough and smart and in control of her own life, or, well, afterlife.

When I tongued the mirror, I didn't imagine another human on the other side. I imagined I was kissing my own ghost.

Amber tasted like pickles that Monday, and I wondered what she'd eaten for lunch, was aroused by the sour smell and taste. I liked that she didn't bother to brush her teeth before coming over. I suddenly wanted every bit of her all at once.

The sunset inked the bedroom walls deep orange, and shards of light burst in the reflection of Amber's glasses. I slid my hands off her hips and reached for her face. She pulled back so quickly I almost fell forward.

"No," she said. "We have to talk. Now."

My hands, which had been seconds away from removing her glasses, hovered between us awkwardly.

"Shoot," I said, pocketing my hands.

"There's something I haven't told you about my parents."

My first thought was that she'd lied to me about being out to her parents, something I could probably deal with but wasn't ideal. I liked secrets, but I didn't want to be one. But it wasn't that. I didn't fully register what she'd said at first. I was still thinking about her pickled breath. I was still thinking about open mouths and the things that spill out of them. I suddenly wished I could place my hand over her mouth while I fucked her into nightfall. Hot breath and spit dampening my palm.

"I had a sister," Amber said. "She died on a family camping trip when I was six and she was four. Drowned."

It was, to say the least, not at all what I expected.

It was, to say the least, strange timing. She was topless. I was still tightly wound with arousal. You might think a dead sister is an instant mood killer, but I'm always at my stupidest when horny, and my mind was slow to shift gears in that bizarre and decidedly unsexy moment. She'd delivered the words as if they were scripted: carefully memorized and rote. Unfeeling. I said nothing. I wondered if I might be dreaming, touched her wrist as if that could provide an answer. Her skin was ice cold. She shivered at my touch, and I decided it wasn't a dream at all.

Strange timing in-fucking-deed. There were plenty of other times she could have mentioned her dead sister. Like, for example, when I'd told her about *my* dead sister. Luci, my funny and loud sister who loved thin-patty cheeseburgers and listening to the scores of movies she'd never seen and making up ghost stories that were as romantic as they were terrifying. Luci, who once had sore legs for three days because

8

she'd spent so many hours bending over to collect seashells at the beach. Luci, who died when she was thirty-two and I was twenty-six. Four years ago, but I prefer to count the time in days, like an astronaut lost in space dictating a diary so they don't go completely insane. 1,464 days since contact with mission control. 1,464 days since my big sister died alone in a car accident.

I looked at Amber and her outline blurred, the room fogged over as if someone had let the outside in. The lowering sun bruised the walls purple now. The room looked dark, and I felt swallowed by it. I closed my eyes and reopened them, but the fog lingered.

"It's okay," Amber said. "I'm okay."

I still hadn't spoken. A phantom fingertip drew a line down my face and I realized it was a tear. I dabbed at my face with my wrists and Amber came into focus. She thought I was crying for her dead sister, not mine.

Finally sex was far from my mind, even with Amber's goosebumped tits staring at me. But this was more than a gear-switch. I mentally overcorrected, swerving toward a guardrail I wasn't sure would hold. I was sad about Luci, a familiar enough feeling for the past 1,464 days, but the sadness clashed with a new feeling. Amber had never lied to me before. And maybe this wasn't an outright lie, but it was a rather large omission. One I couldn't understand.

"Why didn't you tell me?" I asked.

Guilt hit as soon as the words left my mouth. I knew I was making it about me when really this belonged to her. Amber's life. Amber's loss.

I slid my hand over the thin scar on her shoulder. I'd noticed it the first time we slept together but never asked about it, never even wondered really. I didn't see the point of explaining old wounds. I'd never wanted to be the type of person who shared everything with a partner. Amber and I had separate homes, separate cars. We met because she worked in the library at the university, but we had different friend groups on campus. I liked it that way. Sharing some things but not everything. Maybe this was like that, something Amber didn't want to share with me, something she didn't like to share with anyone.

"I don't like to talk about it," Amber said.

I nodded. The space between us couldn't have been more than a foot, but it felt vast in the growing darkness. I pulled her in for a hug. She was so icy, and for a moment I thought I might not be able to focus again, might be back to thinking about all the ways I wanted to make her body warm, to make it quake. She sniffled, and I released her. But she wasn't crying. She stood there, half-naked, studying me, perhaps trying to actually read my mind since I still wasn't offering much by way of words. I took her hand and pulled her to the bed. We sat on its edge, our shoulders touching.

It was hard not to think of my dead sister. It was hard not to think of all the ways I was a bad girl-friend. The former was a near constant, and the latter had become a recurring theme. Just a few days earlier (see, I knew I was starting this in the wrong place), I'd written a list in my journal quite literally labeled Reasons I'm A Bad Girlfriend. A past therapist had gotten me into the habit of making lists, though to be fair, I think she had intended for it to be more of a grounding technique than an exercise in self-loathing.

"My parents are going to talk about it when you see them," Amber said. She spoke softly to the wall in front of us, and I watched her lips. "I had to tell you before our trip."

"Okay," I said.

At the top of the list: *I don't know if I love her*

Under that, in smaller script: *haha what IS love?*

"They talk about it *a lot*," Amber told the wall. "They never really got over it."

"How could they?" I asked.

I meant it. My parents split after Luci died. The divorce was good for them. They were more functional in its aftermath. They were still both people who lost a daughter, sure, so forever changed, never exactly who they were before. But my mother cried less after the divorce. My father joined a grief group and made friends for the first time in his adult life. When they were together, their combined pain choked them silent. They barely spoke—to me or to anyone. So I welcomed their split. Somehow it made more sense to explode the family once Luci was gone than to try to piece anything together.

When my sister died, I died too. Not a piece of me, as another therapist gently suggested. The whole me. I became my ghost self on the other side of the mirror, the one who felt nothing. Who could only stare back passively.

"She drowned," Amber said.

I didn't point out she was repeating herself. I looked at Amber's mouth, her lips parted and soft, and imagined it filling with water, choking her, spilling out into the room and swallowing us up. I saw it so clearly I may as well have been dreaming.

I suppose there's no right way to talk about death. I'd waited until my second date with Amber to tell her about Luci. I'd brought it up on enough first dates to know the woman sitting across from me would always say the wrong thing, because there really is no right thing to say. And then she would feel awkward and I would work overtime to make it feel less awkward, putting on the exhausting My Sister Is Dead But I Promise I'm Still Extremely Fuckable variety show. But the night still usually ended with a weird dance of feelings and apologies rather than the fleshy, sweaty ending I craved.

So I'd successfully avoided my dead sister on the first date with Amber. We went to a taproom on campus, and she wore a pencil skirt and a pink silk shirt, and I made some stupid joke about sexy librarians, knowing she was one from her profile. She humored me by laughing. Two beers in, she placed a hand on my thigh and I knew where the night was headed. She looked good, better than her pictures even. I was immediately attracted to her. That's something that would never end up on the Bad Girlfriend list. Even when I doubted my love for Amber, I never doubted that attraction.

But this *was* on the list: *I objectify her like she's a librarian Barbie*

I didn't talk about my sister on that first date, but now I can't recall what we'd talked about at all. Once she touched my thigh like that, a touch that left no room for ambiguity, I didn't care what we talked about because I knew I'd get what I wanted. I asked Amber out on a date for the same reason I used to hit on women at the only gay bar in town two, sometimes three nights a week, a lot of them undergrads, which I probably should have felt worse about, but it's not like I was their professor. I asked Amber out because in the 1,464 days-and-counting since my sister died, the only times I ever felt truly alive were when I was having sex. It muted the nightmares. It pinpricked my numb skin back to life.

Sure, sex as a coping mechanism wasn't exactly a novel concept. I knew it was a cliché, really. But that's what death always felt like to me, one big fucking cliché. A constant contradiction, too. I felt isolated and unknowable in my loss, but I'd been to enough meetings, sessions, appointments, read enough advice columns, books, and articles to know that everything I felt had been felt by others. Grief feels unique, but it never is. My hyperactive sex drive wasn't special, but I couldn't expect anyone to possibly understand, not really. I saw it as a curse, but I also didn't want anyone to lift it. It was the one haunting I'd grown used to.

On my second date with Amber, I let her in. We went to a dark restaurant this time. She ate grilled trout, and I ate clam linguine with extra parmesan. Between bites, I told her about my dead sister. Not because it was something I needed her to know right then and there. I was still under the impression things would stay casual between us. I only had room for casual. But I told her about Luci simply because the clamshells reminded me of my sister and her sore legs after foraging on the beach.

I didn't need to say she was dead, it just spilled out.

There in the mouth of my bedroom, I tried to think back to how she'd reacted, but I hadn't really given her time to react, had I? Again, I remembered what Amber wore: dark jeans and a green sweater. I remembered how she ate some pieces of her trout with her fingers and how I wanted to suck them. But I couldn't remember how she responded when I told her my sister was dead, if she'd said any of the things people say like *sorry* or if she'd placed a hand over mine. It wouldn't have been the kind of touch I was looking for.

It hadn't scared her off though. A second date became a third became a fourth. This was easier, I realized. It hadn't been the plan to start dating anyone, but the more I thought about it, the more it made sense. Being with Amber would be easier than scouring campus for women to lose myself in. In the safe confines of a committed relationship, I didn't have to think too hard about my cravings.

Amber sniffled, and I forced myself back into the present. This undoubtedly belonged on the Bad Girlfriend list: *I'm making her dead sister about me and my dead sister.* Too busy wandering the corridors of my own grief to be there for Amber when she needed me. She had taken me so off guard, I wanted to rewind, reset.

Amber leaned her head on my shoulder, and I shifted to accommodate.

"It's why I go home every October," she said.

I rubbed her bare back and wished I could give her her shirt but couldn't recall exactly where I'd flung it. Her bra sat in a lump on the floor, a lacy red thing. This was all wrong.

"It's when she died."

I kept rubbing her back and kissed her head. It hadn't occurred to me to ask about last year's October trip. We'd only been dating a month, and families have their things, their little rituals, so I'd assumed this was one of theirs. In a way, I was correct. It *was* ritual. A mourning ritual. Her family had been gathering every year for nearly three decades to remember someone they'd only known a few years. The sludgy sadness of it snapped my brain into focus. I stopped thinking about myself and of Luci. Who cared if it took Amber a year to tell me? She was telling me now, and I needed to be there for her. I owed her so much.

"The good news," I told her, "is I'm great with grief. Like, certified professional over here."

She laughed. Her hair brushed my cheek, and I kissed her head again. And again. I squeezed her, and one of my hands grazed her nipple. That's all it took. My mind switched gears again. Back to sex, the flash of fantasy, placing my hand on her mouth before she could utter anything horrible. My skin was still post-jog slick. I thought of her mouth on the sweatiest, most pungent parts of me. Even in the growing darkness, I saw the faint scar on her shoulder and wanted to trace it with my tongue.

Was it my fault she hadn't told me about her dead sister? Did I ask her enough about herself when we first started dating? Was it bad that I remembered what she wore to dates better than what we talked about? Of course it was bad. It belonged on the Bad Girlfriend list for sure.

I wondered, not for the first time, if I was a love grifter. Sometimes I felt like I loved Amber, but love was like a shiny lure at the end of a fishhook. Something soft sutured to something sharp. A trap.

Here she was, opening up to me, and I couldn't stop thinking about her open legs.

"What was her name?" I asked.

"Helen," she said.

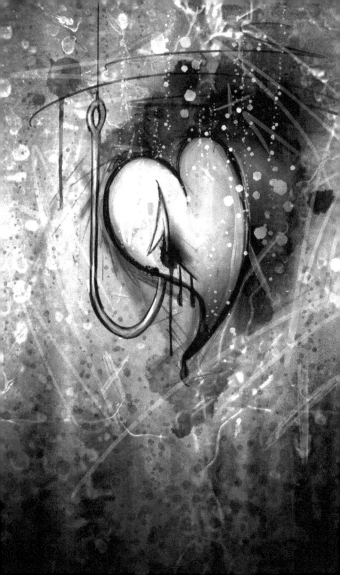

I kissed her shoulder. "Helen," I echoed. "Pretty."

Amber nuzzled into me and didn't say anything more.

Her breath was slow and heavy, and for a moment I wondered if she'd fallen asleep.

Then I felt it. Her hand on my waist. It wasn't freezing like her skin before. It was warm and urgent, the same way she'd touched me on our first date. I could feel her needing me, and this was a need I could answer.

Amber twisted on top of me and pulled my hand toward her. We had good but quick, quiet sex and then she fell asleep for real. Things felt right again, for a moment.

In the morning, I found the grape shapes of three bruises on my upper arm, left behind by Amber's fingers. She'd gripped me there, hard. During sex or while we slept, I wasn't sure. It was as if she'd been worried she'd float away.

I willed myself to be what she needed, silently vowed to stay by her side even though I could already feel myself pulling away. I didn't yet know how far this vow would take me, how lost in someone else's ghost story I'd become.

AMBER'S PARENTS LIVED all the way at the top of the state, too far to drive and far enough from the closest airport that we had to rent a car. I wanted to get a truck, and Amber poked fun at me for being a city girl with a stereotypical idea of life up north.

Amber drove the Bronco, winding along curvy roads cut around lakes, lined by trees with leaves gone orange, yellow, and red, deeper hues than the ones that swept across campus every fall, as if there was an entirely different saturation setting up here.

"Those red ones," I said, placing a finger on the cool window glass. "They look like maraschino cherries. These colors, wow."

Amber laughed.

"You really do sound like a city girl," she said. "It's not even peak yet. You haven't seen nothing."

But I couldn't imagine them getting *more* beautiful. With a pang, I thought of Amber's sister. Her death fell so close to peak fall, a dark cloud muting the brightest time of year. Amber turned up the radio and I wondered if she was thinking about the same thing.

A part of me felt closer to her. We were both card-carrying members of the Dead Sisters Club, decidedly less sexy than the Dead Wives Club, and less damaged than the Dead Moms Club. The love I'd been doubting firmed up into something more grippable. The guilt I felt for using Amber as an escape hatch for the entirety of our relationship evaporated. Love was hard, but loss I knew.

And sure, our losses weren't twinned. Not even sis-ters really. More like distant cousins. I was an adult when Luci died. Amber had been so young when Helen died. What happens to a child when death makes its imprint so early on? If Helen's death had fractured Amber in some lasting way, I couldn't see it. She seemingly carried less emotional baggage than any other woman I'd been with. Hadn't I been drawn to her for precisely this reason? She was hot and uncomplicated. Or, at least, good at hiding her complications. Or maybe I was bad at seeing them.

As we neared our destination, Amber drifted. I placed my hand on her thigh, but she kept both hands on the wheel. I traced small circles on her leg, but she didn't react. This is a trap I fall into with myself often. Needing a woman to react to my touch, to stay here and close. But not *too* close. When people drift away from me, I get twitchy, desperate to draw them back in. All I needed was for Amber to look at me, to place her hand on mine, something to show she wanted me to be there. Nothing. I took my hand off, and I swear I could sense her body relax. It made me mad. And then guilty for getting mad.

Amber plugged in her phone and let the same album loop and loop, either not noticing or not caring. It was something poppy about heartbreak, the kind of sadness that's kind of pretty. I hummed along and stared out at the lakes, wondering if my girlfriend feared big, cold bodies of water, knowing this was something I should already know. It was our first time existing together outside our ten miles of campus and town. It could be good to get to know her better here, removed, on her turf, away from our usual contexts. Maybe I could let her know me a little more, too.

Not too much, of course.

At last we pulled up to a brown A frame sitting a mile back from the main road. Amber's parents were outside waving. They looked like postcard people. It's not like I'd been expecting to find her parents dressed in all black. It's not like I'd been expecting a haunted house by the lake. But Amber had spoken about her parents as if there'd be something obviously wrong with them. And here was her father, tall and lean and blonde, wearing dark jeans and red flannel like a handsome lumberjack. He had his arm around her mother, who looked exactly like Amber. The same nose that lilted slightly to the left, the same thick dark hair pulled back in a ponytail. She wore a cashmere red sweater over cream colored pants. Their ordinary clothes, the big house, their toothy smiles, it all surprised me. They looked happy. They looked normal, much more normal than my parents.

Amber parked and turned off the car, the looped album finally cutting off. Outside, cold wind whipped my hair. The air smelled like damp leaves and burning wood, like we'd stepped into their postcard. Pam and Arnold Stevenson introduced themselves at once, each holding out a hand. Handshakers, not huggers. I tucked this piece of information inside my mental file folder for Girlfriend's Parents. I was going to be good this weekend. I was going to learn about them and, in turn, learn about Amber, do the kind of relationship work I should have done in the beginning. Better late than never.

"I'll get those," Arnold said, reaching for the bags.

"No, no," I said. Normally, I took men up on these offers, which always made me feel guilty, like I was a bad dyke somehow for letting a strong man do things for me. But some part of me wanted Pam and Arnold to know I could take care of their daughter, that she was safe with me. That was true, wasn't it? As much as I used her, I wasn't harming her, not actively, I don't think. What do you think, am I allowed to ask that?

I struggled with our bags. I should have taken Arnold up on his offer. My joints were stiff from the drive, and the cold air made my knuckles ache.

"Still know your way or did you have to use a GPS?" Pam asked.

"Mom," Amber said in exasperation.

"Just teasing," Pam said. "You know I just wish you came out more often."

Pam put her arm around Amber's shoulders, and Amber held her mom's back. They walked like that, arm-in-arm.

"Your hair's different," Pam said.

"I know, I'm sorry, I meant to tell you I got it cut."

It was an odd thing to apologize for, but I didn't read too much into it. I knew daughters sometimes

had these kinds of relationships with their mothers. A tugging, like they were trying to consume one another. Luci had been that way with our mom, always fighting about stupid things like what she wore and who she hung out with. I'd always been allowed to get away with murder.

Pam and Amber walked up the front stairs, still embraced, and I looked up at them before ascending, watched them hover above me with their backs turned and heads curved toward each other. They looked like garden statues. Pam had the same tiny ears as Amber. I teased Amber about them sometimes—*how can you even hear with those!*—but I also liked to lick them during sex because she once told me it makes her wet. *Like all at once*, she'd said, *like flicking on a sprinkler*. Watching her entwined with her mother, the two of them like past and future versions of each other, I slipped away to some other place, my mind full of, well, no. There's no fucking way I'm telling you, not yet, you don't have all the pieces, and it won't make sense. Let's just say Pam and Amber looked sweet, and I briefly missed my mother, though I couldn't imagine us ever walking arm-in-arm.

I stopped at the doorstep. The handle of Amber's bag dug into my palm's flesh, and I had a strong urge not to enter, the back of my throat dry, the way it sometimes was when I woke up from nightmares.

Amber disentangled from Pam, who followed Arnold over the threshold into their house.

"Hey," Amber said. "What's wrong?"

She tugged on my sleeve, and her touch pulled me back.

"Nothing," I said. "Just tired from the drive."

"Dad can put on some coffee," Amber said.

I nodded and followed her inside.

As soon as we stepped through the door, I was bowled over by the dramatic temperature change. It was hot. Very hot. It felt like someone or something was huffing their fevered breath on me. My skin didn't know how to react. I shivered.

Amber must have felt what I did, because she said playfully: "Oh, I should have told you to bring a bathing suit. These two like to feel like they're living in a sauna." She thumbed Pam and Arnold, who waved their hands in over-performed denial. It looked like an act they'd been through plenty of times. Another script.

"Nothing wrong with wanting to escape the cold," Pam said. Amber looked so much like Pam there wasn't any Arnold in her at all. I wondered if Helen looked like him.

BY NIGHTTIME, I WAS SWEATING through my clothes. I was a little annoyed with Amber for not warning me about the heat. I would have packed more tanks and fewer sweaters. I cracked a window in the room where we were staying, Amber's childhood room, which didn't bear many traces of her girlhood. Her parents had converted it into a neutral lakeside cabin-themed guest room in the A's peak. Amber closed the window. She said Pam would notice. Like any good girlfriend, I wanted to please the parents, and I knew Amber was anxious about this trip. I didn't try to open the window again.

The first mention of Helen came while we were still alone, sweating together in that little room. Amber moved her folded clothes from her suitcase to a dresser, a process entirely too laborious for a few-days trip, but I thought it was cute. I suddenly couldn't wait to fuck her in her childhood bedroom and wondered if it'd be her first time doing so. Who else had she brought to this looming A frame in the woods?

We were expected downstairs for dinner soon, so sex, even if we were quiet, the thought of which turned me on even more goddamnit, was out of the question. I needed a distraction. I flopped onto the bed, compelled to strip off the blankets. It was so goddamn hot. I glanced at Amber from behind, still sorting her clothes into neat piles, as if she were moving in, her ass hugged by a pair of unfairly sheer yoga pants. I took my phone out to text someone, anyone. But there was no service. I asked Amber for the wifi password and she hesitated. She turned, and I saw a look in her face I hadn't seen since she told me about Helen.

"It's one of those weird things," she said.

"Like a lot of random numbers?"

"No. It's Helen1017."

"Oh," I said.

"I know. It's weird."

I stood and went to her. I could be what she needed me to be, just like she could be what I needed her to be.

I held her, kissed her soft, warm cheeks flushed with the sweltering heat of the home she grew up in, sisterless.

"It's not weird," I told her, and I meant it.

We all do things to keep the dead with us. I opened my wallet and pulled out the seashell that's always there. Round and smooth and pale yellow with a glossy pink interior. The size of a penny. I pressed it in Amber's hand and didn't need to explain what it was or who it belonged to. I knew she would know, and I was grateful for the shorthand.

DINNER WAS NORMAL until it wasn't. The dining room, big and pristine like something out of a museum, smelled like juniper berries and port. Pam served pan-fried morel mushrooms and roast pheasant with bread sauce. We drank red wine. I had either grown used to the heat or was tipsy enough not to mind.

"You're in a program?" Arnold asked me. He sat at one end of the table, Pam at the other. Amber and I sat together on one of the table's sides. It was an odd arrangement, one whole side of the table empty.

"I'm working on my dissertation right now," I said.

"About?"

I stabbed a spongey mushroom on my plate. It's

always difficult to suss out exactly how openminded straight people my parents' ages are, no offense to you if, well, I don't know how old you are.

"It's about coded queerness in Victorian gothic literature," I said. I ate the mushroom. "But also modern gay arthouse pornography that engages with the fantastic."

Arnold raised his eyebrows. But to my surprise, he was genuinely interested—or good at feigning it.

"Vampires seems like an obvious one," Arnold said.

"Oh, yeah, lots of homoerotics in the vampire stuff," I said, slicing into my bird and taking a bite. "But really, all monsters are gay."

"That's a worrisome trope though, isn't it?" Arnold said. "To make gay people out to be monsters?"

"Well, it can be, but I'm trying to complicate that, too."

He asked me a string of questions, and he nodded as I spoke, added some of his own insight even. Amber had told me Arnold worked in landscaping, so his interest in my work surprised me, which I suppose was another one of my rural assumptions coming through, like with the truck. Arnold was easy to talk to, warm but a little prodding, like he was challenging me, but in a good way, not some macho game. He was different from my own father, who was quiet and calm, not a bad dad by any means, but hard to reach, even when we were right next to each other. My dad *did* have a PhD and never asked me about my dissertation. To be fair, the sex parts would mortify him.

"Did you just say the words *postcolonial theories of sexuality* to my dad?" Amber asked, and everyone laughed. I realized I hadn't included her in the conversation, in fact I'd turned away from her to face Arnold, but she'd seemed busy talking to Pam about something else.

"I guess I did!" I said, shifting back toward her. "I see where your librarian brain comes from."

It got quiet. Amber took her hand off my knee. She did this sometimes. Hot and cold. Belly-laughing one second, stone silent the next, and no map for me to understand how she got from one to the other. Whenever I'd ask what was wrong, her answer was always the same: *nothing*. So I stopped asking.

"And how *is* work for you?" Arnold asked, breaking the silence, which couldn't have been much longer than a few seconds but felt drawn out.

"It's good," she said.

"The promotion was exciting," I added, taking another swig of wine.

Pam and Arnold looked at me, confused. I looked at Amber, confused.

"Oh, right, yes, I forgot to tell you," she said. "I'm working interlibrary loan now."

"It came with a big raise," I said. I was proud of Amber. She worked hard and cared about the students who often took library work for granted even though they depended on it. When she found out about the promotion, we'd gone out for Korean BBQ. Later in bed, I could still smell the smoke in her hair, and it made me hungry for her. I mean, sure, I was always hungry for her. But that smoky smell was like a spell, and I asked her to put on the harness I usually wore, watched her fumble with its buckles and straps without offering any assistance, my hunger deepening when she whispered, *Like this?*

I was puzzled by why Amber hadn't told them about the promotion yet, but I was more puzzled by their reaction. Pam and Arnold's warmth leaked away. It was as if they'd been told their daughter had quit her stable library job to pursue professional clowning. Pam nodded, but she didn't look up from the spindly, naked pheasant bones on her plate. Arnold forced a smile, and I decided, no, he wasn't good at acting after all. The silence was larger in the heat. I noticed the walls sweating condensation behind Arnold's head. It was odd, the walls so slick and glistening. Was it because it was so cold outside? Did they have a leak? Was I seeing it right? I wanted to reach out and touch the wall. Maybe it would be cold, a relief.

Pam turned to me and smiled brightly, a flipped switch. "I hope you like the room," she said. "I'm sorry the guest house wasn't done in time."

"Guest house?" I asked. Amber's hand found my knee again, which made me relax, but she squeezed, hard, and I wasn't sure what it meant. I gulped my wine.

"You probably didn't see it when we drove in," Amber said. "It's back in the woods behind the house. Kind of hidden."

"Amber loved that little house," Pam said.

"I guess I did," Amber said.

"The renovation was supposed to be done this summer, but you know how those things go," Arnold said. I didn't, but I nodded. "We're going to call it Helen House when it's done," he added.

"Dad," Amber said.

"Oh," I said, hoping to diffuse any tension before it could settle in. "Amber told me about Helen."

"Do you have any siblings?" Pam asked.

"I did. An older sister. But she died, too. Four years ago." *1,478 days*, I said to myself.

"Well, fuck," Pam said, and it surprised me so much I laughed. Her sudden vulgarity was an unexpected and probably unintended bit of comedy, but it also hit me right in the heart. Maybe there *is* a right response to someone else's grief. Maybe it's a simple *fuck*.

"Sorry," I said, still laughing. "I'm used to people saying things like 'I'm sorry to hear that' or 'what a shame.'"

"Well, I *am* sorry about it," Pam said. "But I also know being sorry doesn't change anything. She's still gone. And it's fucking awful."

I laughed. There it was again. That word. It was the exact right thing to say.

"I think grief counselors could learn a fucking thing or two from you," I said, and for a moment I worried

I'd overshot it, but then all three of them laughed. Arnold had to put his fork down he was laughing so hard. Pam laughed with her mouth full of food, flecks of pheasant meat in her teeth. She snorted a little. Amber grabbed my hand as she laughed, her grip gentle now.

"I guess I could have said *monster fucking* when talking about my thesis after all," I said. Another chorus of laughter. I was nailing this.

I ONCE AGREED TO GO with my father to his support group. It wasn't just for fathers who'd lost children, as I'd believed. All kinds of mourners were present— widows and widowers, old folks whose friends were dying in waves, people with ghosts for siblings, friends, cousins, lovers. There were so many kinds of death. "A bereavement mix pack," I joked in the car after, and I was pleased when my dad laughed, a rare sound from this man who was quiet even before Luci died.

At the meeting, I found myself relating most to the widowers. It was another truth I kept locked inside me with my curse. When these men talked about their gone wives, I thought about my sister. They kept talking about the feeling of coming home to an empty house, of turning on lights expecting to see their wives sprung back from the dead. One man said he'd leave on faucets just to feel like someone else was in the house, would fill a tub with water and never get in, the sound reminding him of how his wife used to run a bath every Sunday evening. Another said he'd found a video online of just a woman going through her morning routine—washing her face, putting on makeup, brushing her teeth, no commentary at all, just ambient getting-ready sounds. ASMR crap. But for him, an escape hatch. He confessed he put it on every morning.

Empty houses. I hadn't lived with Luci since we were children. And yet I knew exactly what these men were talking about. Spaces felt either too big or too small, the proportions of my home Wonderlanded and wrong. I was always flipping on light switches hoping the shadows would take on new shape. Luci didn't live with me when we were adults, yet she was always with me in the apartment, chattering away on FaceTime while I cooked fish curry, helping me pick out what to wear on dates (back when I actually cared about dating for the right reasons), texting me strings of missives from the various jobs she worked, most of them outside because Luci wasn't an indoor kid like me. She liked dirt and trees and collecting parts of the earth—seashells and rocks and bleached animal bones. She didn't have to literally be inside my house for me to feel like she was always there, always a text away.

Yes, I understood these men and the pain of empty houses. We were not the same, and yet we were knotted together.

AFTER DINNER, I BROUGHT THE DISHES to Pam in the kitchen and offered to dry them. She handed me a faded blue dishtowel. We chatted while we did the dishes, and everything was normal and pleasant once more, Amber perched on a stool beside us, watching. When we finished, Pam said she had something to show me, and Amber stayed behind to play cribbage with her father.

Pam led me to the back of the house's first floor, and I knew we were going to Helen's old room without having to be told. I wasn't afraid or put off. I wondered if there was a slight psychic connection between those who have lost. I hadn't seen it in Amber until she told me, but Pam radiated something I recognized.

Pam opened a door, but it didn't lead to exactly what I expected. Yes, this had been Helen's room, maybe even a room she and Amber shared as little ones, on the same floor as the master, much easier for parents to watch over them, keep them safe. I knew in my bones Helen had slept here. But the room bore no resemblance to a nursery or child's room. I'd imagined a taxidermied room, carefully preserved by Pam and Arnold, containing a colorful bedspread and finger-painted art and barely used toys. But it was just a room. All traces of history sluiced away just like Amber's old room.

What Pam wanted to show me wasn't the room itself but something it contained. She went to the closet and pulled down a large box draped in a dust cloth. When she pulled off the cloth, I saw it wasn't a box but an actual dollhouse. A large, lovely pale blue nineteenth century manor shrunk down to play-size but every bit as detailed as the real thing.

"I thought you might like this," Pam said. "Because your dissertation. The gothic stuff."

She motioned for me to turn off the lights. I followed her orders as unquestioningly as I'd followed her to this strange, lifeless room. I hit the light switch

and heard Pam fumbling in the dark before something clicked it into place. Suddenly, the dollhouse
glowed.

"There," Pam said.

Lights flickered in every window, casting tiny
shadows across its walls and halls. Every bedroom
had its own color scheme, carved wooden four-
poster beds draped in quilts and puffy pillows. A
miniature clawfoot bathtub stood in one of the
bathrooms, its feet brushed gold. A wood stove the
size of a fat cherry tomato burned in the kitchen.
The dollhouse's little lights looked impossibly like
real candlelight. It really was magnificent.

"Amber told me it was a car accident," Pam said.
She looked at the house as she talked, like Amber
had looked at the wall when telling me about Helen.
Sometimes it's easier to talk to a house than the
people inside it. "Do people say just horrible things
to you and think they're being nice?" Pam asked.

I nodded even though she wasn't looking at me.
"At least it was quick, at least she didn't suffer," I said,
taking on the high-pitched cadence of performed
sympathy.

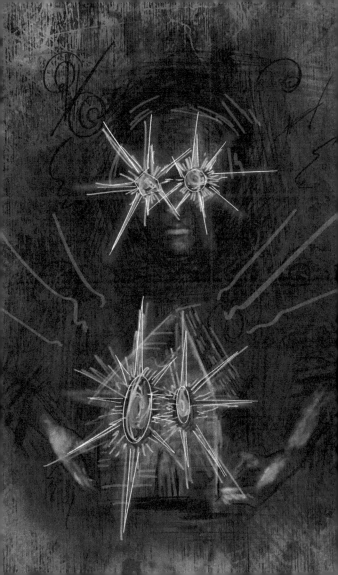

Pam laughed. "People love to talk about how drowning is supposedly a calm experience," she said. "They always read it in a book."

"Fuck that," I said, and Pam laughed.

She touched the roof of the dollhouse and then jerked back her hand as if it had burned her. A swirl of smoke coiled out of the dollhouse's chimney, and I marveled at the engineering of this little thing, figured it must have cost a fortune. I stared, transfixed. The windows seemed to fog, the glass blurring, but I blinked and they looked normal again. I reminded myself it was just a toy. An elaborate one, but a toy all the same. I looked at Pam, but she wouldn't take her eyes off the house.

"My mom never really grasped the concept of sympathy casseroles," I said. "She thought they were disgusting."

"I don't think she was calm," Pam said.

"Hmm?"

"Helen," Pam said. She must not have heard me about the casseroles.

"I think she was cold."

"Put it away," a voice said from behind us, and I jumped. Even with the dollhouse glowing, it was still dark, and I squinted at the doorframe where someone hovered. Bright spots danced in my vision from the flickering miniature lights. The real room's light came back on, and Amber stood in the doorway. "Please, mom, please make this easy," she said.

"It's okay," I said. "Really, it's fine."

"You don't know what you're talking about," Amber said, and she fled. I followed her, pausing only to give a quick apologetic smile to Pam, who was still watching the dollhouse flicker.

As I chased after Amber, I realized there were no pictures on the walls, none of Helen, none of Amber. Just the occasional generic wall piece from a home goods store, things like a wire metal sailboat and a wooden sign that read **LAKE LIFE** in faded letters. We may as well have been in a vacation rental, welcoming but staged. The whole house seemed less lived-in and more lived-on, like the Stevensons were dolls placed there by some invisible hand.

I DESPERATELY WANTED to open a window. I sat sweating on the floor in the oven masquerading as a bedroom, feeling like the roasted witch in Hansel & Gretel, and oh, how that story reminded me of Luci. I tried to push it away.

Amber wasn't crying. She was pacing, balling her hands into tiny fists and releasing them over and over. I couldn't imagine standing in the heat, let alone moving. I'd taken my shirt off, and realized I was now the one weirdly topless during a serious conversation.

"I shouldn't have brought you here," she said. She didn't sound angry. She sounded afraid. But I dismissed her with a wave.

"I think you *need* me here," I said. "Your parents seem to upset you."

"How could they not?" Amber laughed. "I know you're trying to help," she said. "I love you for it. I've never brought someone home. I worried my parents would be, well, *them*. And it's fine when it's just me. But they get even worse around other people I think. But then with you. They wanted me to bring you. They're obsessed with you, you know."

I did not know this, and how could I have? Amber hadn't mentioned her parents until that one night. When had Amber even told them about me, and what had she said? I liked that they liked me. I liked that I could be something nice for them, for their daughter. But obsessed with me? It seemed extreme. Already, I could feel myself loosening, pulling away from Amber. Things were moving fast, freaky fast.

"I thought maybe you'd understand them," Amber said. "Since you lost someone, too."

"Hey," I said. It felt too hot to say much more than that.

"I'm being so selfish," Amber said.

"Hey, hey, hey," I said, and I reached for her hands and pulled her down to me. She squatted and seeing her there in front of me, I willed myself to not drift away, to be there for her.

"Have they done therapy?" I asked. "Or like have you done it together? As a family?"

"Forever ago," Amber said, the wine from dinner on her breath. I thought the alcohol might be heightening her emotions. It was rare for her to be this worked up, this visibly rattled. But I *had* seen it before. Usually after a few drinks. Usually when those drinks were medicating a stressful day at work. She couldn't sit in those moments, had to pace even if we were in a crowded bar. I'd learned to identify the signs, especially since those were the times we were most likely to argue. But she was also impulsive and wild in those moments in a way I was drawn to. She was impulsive and wild in those moments in a way that reminded me of Luci.

"The therapy didn't stop them," Amber said.

"Didn't stop what?"

Amber paused, and I could see her doing calculations in her head. Deciding if this was another thing to share or to keep as hers. *Tell me*, I thought, willing grief telepathy to be a real thing. *This can be ours.*

"The nightmares."

I knew about post-death nightmares. I'd been seized by them in the immediate aftermath of Luci's death. Not even particularly imaginative ones. My brain kept it simple: car crash after car crash after car crash. It got to the point where sometimes dreams that had nothing to do with Luci would be interrupted by a blinding pair of headlights. Crash, crash, crash. Complete and total destruction. Exactly how I felt in my waking life unless I had another body to crash into.

"I have nightmares, too," I said.

"No," Amber said. "You don't understand."

Of course I understood the impulse to make your own grief sound different, special, unknowable.

But Amber frustrated me with this whole *you don't understand* business, and that frustration pulled at the edges of my desire to be a good and loving and less selfish girlfriend.

"I think I do, I have—"

"We don't just have nightmares," she said. "We all have the *same* nightmares."

"What?"

"Same exact ones as each other. Like we're all in them at the same time."

"Shared nightmares?" I asked. My throat went dry, and my legs locked into place. I felt caught in beaming headlights, something big and fast rounding a corner. I closed my eyes as if bracing for actual impact, but only felt a slow tickle down my back, a bead of sweat rolling, like silk pulled across flesh.

"Shared nightmares, shared night terrors," Amber said. "Sometimes we used to sleepwalk during them. Sleeprun, really. Because Helen would be chasing us, torturing us. It's how I got this." She touched the scar on her shoulder. "I was trying to run away from Helen. She was chasing me with a grape peeler. My mother used to peel grapes for us to take to the lake, because she worried we'd choke on the skins. Helen got to me in the nightmare, and she peeled each of my toes one by one, and I couldn't wake up. When I did, I was in the hallway. I'd run into a wall, and a picture frame had fallen and cut me. There was blood everywhere."

"In the dream?" I said.

"No, no, the grape peeler was in the dream, but the picture frame and the wall happened in real life. When I woke up, dad was on the floor, crawling, like his legs didn't work. I tripped on him I think, and it woke him up, too. Mom was still asleep though, slamming drawers in the kitchen like she was looking for something."

"The grape peeler?"

"No Helen had the grape peeler, so I dunno, a weapon. Something to fight her off with probably."

"Helen had the grape peeler in the dream though, not in real life," I said.

"I know that. I know that," Amber said. "We were too scared to wake up my mom, because what if she came at us thinking we were Helen? So my dad got up and threw a glass of water in her face, and she came to. I had to get a bunch of stitches. They made me promise I wouldn't tell the doctors about the dream or any of it."

"Your parents made you promise that?"

"Yes!"

I could either cry or scream. Something else told me to choose neither and, instead, run. But I stayed put.

"You don't believe me do you?" Amber asked.

"No, I do, I do," I said. And it was the truth. I believed her, because it had to be true, because it was so horribly fucked.

"We don't get them as often anymore," Amber said. "Only sometimes. On really cold nights."

I remembered a time she'd spent the night at my place. It was the first snowy night of last winter. We'd spiked our cocoa with creme de menthe while we watched the snow come down in fat flakes. In the middle of the night, I woke to Amber screaming and had to shake her awake. I didn't ask what her nightmare had been about, probably too concerned with my own dreamscape of screeching brakes and headlight-glow.

"She wants something from us," Amber whispered.

I resisted the annoying academic in my head who wanted to say something about how the vengeful Helen her family dreamed of was a manifestation of their guilt, shame, and trauma. A mental form of self-harm. But I shut the stupid theory bitch up. It wasn't what Amber needed or wanted to hear. So I listened. I opened myself up to Amber. I imagined myself as a pool of hot wax for her to press into, imagined becoming the hard shell she needed to protect herself. She told me about the dreams in detail, more like the grape peeler, some worse. One in which Helen hung Amber, Pam, and Arnold from meat hooks. One in which she set Amber's hair on fire. I told myself it was just like the stories Luci told when we slipped into that otherworld under her quilt late at night. Ghost stories, nothing more. It was the only way I could stomach it.

"She wants her doll," Amber said. "She comes to us in our dreams and always screams for her doll and that fucking dollhouse."

WE WOKE TO THE SMELL of sugar and browned butter. I'd spent the night holding Amber, genuinely worried about her, eventually falling into a sweat-soaked and dreamless sleep. Amber's hair stuck to me. My own hair stuck to me. I peeled myself from her, and she made a sweet sleep sound. I hoped her sleep was dreamless, too.

I took a cold shower and felt some relief, like my melted insides were firming into solids again. I toweled off and looked in the mirror. I appeared tired and a little swollen, the way I look after crying, though I hadn't shed a tear in weeks. I wondered if the heat was doing something to me, to my body. Filling me up. I was tempted to kiss my reflection, as if it might breathe some life back into me.

Instead, I pulled at the mirror's corner. It hinged open, my reflection vanishing. Inside, there were rows and rows of pill bottles, mostly downers. I'd been on benzos, too, in the first few months after Luci's death, when getting in a vehicle without having a panic attack felt impossible. I'd stopped driving myself, took the bus instead, and spent money I didn't have on car services.

I expected the pill bottles to say Pam's name on them, but they didn't. I wondered why Amber would keep all these pills here, in a place she only came to once a year. If she didn't need them, why keep them at all? But I kept mine, I reminded myself. They were right there in my medicine cabinet, unconcealed, because what was there to hide? Amber had probably seen them. I still took them from time to time and had slipped one in my pocket before heading to the airport for this trip, knowing the car ride to Amber's parents' would be long, and though it had been a while since I'd had an anxiety attack in a car, things had felt off recently, and I wanted to be prepared. I'd been so focused on trying to figure out what was going on in Amber's mind I'd forgotten my own fears.

As I looked at the pills, I considered another possibility: If she *did* need them, how hadn't I noticed her taking anything back home? If she had meds she took regularly, I'd know, wouldn't I?

Maybe not.

I was, after all, not the most observant or curious girlfriend.

I was, after all, using Amber.

And I was starting to feel like she was using me. Though I couldn't really parse out for what.

I thought about what she'd told me about the nightmares and how her parents made her lie to the doctors. I wondered if these, too, were something not entirely her choice. Pam and Arnold were nice, not at all stern, but there was something *imposing* about them. Like they wanted Amber to be a certain way. She acted different here, quieter, her hot and cold tendencies more pronounced.

Maybe I could do the thing I should have been doing the whole time and just ask my girlfriend questions. But when I got back to the bedroom, Amber was gone, the bed made, a ritual she performed every morning, even at my place where I told her it wasn't necessary.

I dressed in the least amount of clothes that could be deemed appropriate—a loose t-shirt and black high-waisted skirt—and went down-stairs, where Pam handed me a plate of heart-shaped waffles dusted with powdered sugar.

Amber and Arnold were sitting at the table drinking coffee and eating their waffles. Amber spattered rhubarb jam on hers, and I had a hard time not thinking about blood from peeled toes.

Arnold looked up from his newspaper and folded it as I sat down.

"Ah, wonderful," he said. "I have something for you both."

Amber was tense.

"We don't need to do presents," she said.

"Nonsense." Arnold set his paper down and disappeared.

Pam was still making waffles, stacking them on a plate. She had already made enough for a group three times our size. She hummed over her griddle and looked as if she were in a trance, her movements with the spatula rhythmic and repetitive, her humming not unpleasant but also a little too loud. For the millionth time, I wondered how people could comfortably live in a house this hot. At least my hair was still wet.

Arnold returned to the table with two wrapped boxes, one large, one small. He handed the small one to Amber and nodded for her to open it. She looked nervous as she peeled the brown parchment paper away. Inside was a slim black notebook with her name printed on it in gold lettering. She mumbled a thanks and thumbed through the notebook and didn't make eye contact with me.

Arnold placed a hand on my shoulder. "Now you," he said. When he took his hand away, I felt something cold take its place. Like he'd set an ice pack there. Then it melted away.

I smiled, but like most people, I absolutely loathe the ritual of opening gifts in front of others. As I unwrapped my box, Pam's humming crescendoed. A burning smell filled my nose, and everything just felt

very fucking off. I didn't want to see what was inside the box but wasn't sure how to get out of it now. I opened it, holding my breath. At first, I couldn't tell what it was. It looked like a lace tablecloth.

"Oh wow," I said, buying time. I lifted the soft fabric, and it unfurled. It wasn't a tablecloth. It was a dress. Cream-colored lace with blue pearl buttons. Obscenely gorgeous. It wasn't my style, to say the least, and yet I was seized by a desire to put it on. But I was also seized by the suffocating feeling in this kitchen, in this house, my girlfriend's father gifting me a beautiful and no doubt expensive dress in front of his daughter and his zoned-out, humming wife. I felt dizzy. I felt overheated for real. I needed another cold shower or three.

Amber gawked at the dress, but she looked awed by its beauty, too. Pam abandoned her waffles and quit humming. We all looked at the dress, and I felt like screaming.

"It's beautiful," I said instead, but it came out like a question. I'd been trying to be the good and go-with-the-flow girlfriend, but this was all too much. I didn't know how to make sense of it. I reached for Amber's hand, and she pulled it away but also averted her eyes from the dress. As soon as she did, she clenched her fists and glared at Arnold. I worried for a moment she might actually punch her dad in the face.

"Way to be a total fucking creep, dad," she said. She pushed back from the table and marched off.

"It's beautiful," I repeated, this time with more certainty, but I also knew I was overdoing it, speaking to Arnold like he was a child. He smiled sheepishly and looked down.

I chased after Amber but still clutched the dress. Instead of turning for the stairs, she stomped toward the other side of the house, and I knew where she was headed. I followed her to Helen's bedroom. The dollhouse was still on the floor, its fake candles extinguished so it no longer held the magic it had in the night. It looked like a toy.

"Don't," I said, but it was too late. Amber brought one slippered foot down on the house's roof. That's all it took. The roof caved, and we both knew the dollhouse would never light up again.

"I'm just a little worried," I said. I was trying to keep my voice down, but Amber didn't seem to care.

She was furiously changing her clothes, layering up, and the sight of her sweater made me want to pass out.

"Say it," Amber said. "Say you think we're messed up."

"But I don't."

"You looked so freaked out," she said.

"Well, yeah, you have to admit the dress is a little weird!"

I was still holding it. I didn't want to put it down.

"You could have just said thank you and left it at that," she said.

"I tried to!"

"Aren't you going to ask me about *my* gift?" she asked. She pulled the notebook out of her pocket and threw it in my general direction, though I told myself she didn't know what she was doing.

Despite my curiosity, I didn't want to know about the little black notebook with its gold lettering. It seemed mundane enough, but nothing was as it seemed in this house. I feared answers to any questions at this point. Everything that had felt wrong about Amber's parents, about their house, felt worse the longer I stayed.

I knew for certain now that the empty side of

the table had been reserved for Helen, her presence thick and heavy there. Of course my girlfriend hadn't told me she had a dead sister. Her dead sister was haunting her.

"They gave me a fucking reporter's notebook because they're still hoping I'll become a *reporter* one day."

I didn't know what to do with this information.

"Because *she* wanted to be a reporter," Amber said in a strange, angry whisper. She didn't sound like herself.

"But she was—"

"A toddler when she died?" Amber asked, her voice still quiet but rattling. "Yeah, I fucking know. She used to sit on my dad's lap when he read the newspaper. Somehow that translates to them always thinking she would have become a reporter."

She looked at me expectantly. I couldn't find any words, let alone the right ones. It was beyond unhealthy behavior for her parents to concoct such a fantasy, but Amber already knew this.

"You don't get it at all."

She turned away from me and looked out the window. How could she say this? Any of this? I got it alright. I felt what she felt. Or maybe not exactly. Or maybe *that's* the thing I got. The certainty that no one knows what you're fucking talking about. Those contradictions. Here's what I know I knew then: I knew we were both unwhole. I knew we were the living ones but that we were also the ghosts. I knew death was a sieve, full of holes that can't all be plugged at once. I knew no one else felt my exact pain. Because their someone wasn't my someone. Luci wasn't Helen and Helen wasn't Luci and I wasn't Amber and she wasn't me. But every time I put something into words, it sounds like something that has been said before, like something you could read in a book. There's nothing special about it at all. Yes, everyone's grief is valid. But no, you don't always want to hear about it. Yes, maybe I relate to widowers more than anyone else, but no, I don't want to fucking unpack that. Amber didn't tell me about her dead sister until she had to. I didn't tell her I fuck away the pain, and I never would. I would never tell her I almost ended things the second we started having less sex. I only didn't go through with it because I *did* care about her and *did* get more than sex out of our relationship and couldn't bear to lose her because of my own shit I hadn't even begun to untangle because oh god untangling this shit wouldn't be worrying a knot unloose, it would be another destruction. It would be a razed forest, an extinguished light, do you see what I mean about the clichés? About the failures of language? I kept secrets of my own from Amber. I didn't let her see all of me. I don't even want you to see all of me. You want to see all of me? You sure about that? Here goes. What if I told you when I saw Pam for the first time and realized she looked so much like Amber, I didn't think it was sweet and cute. I thought it was hot. I was attracted to her, even wondered if her lips tasted citrusy like Amber's. I'd literally wanted to fuck my girlfriend's mom upon meeting her. Here's me, here's who I really am. A fucking grief monster. It was much easier to turn everything off and fuck and fantasize about fucking and *fuck* this shit sucks. Pam had it right. Fuck fuck fuckfuckfuckfuck.

A week ago, I would have said something like *help me get it*. But standing there in that hot room in front of a woman I was becoming less certain I actually knew, I was drained. My insides were boiled. Her grief felt too big to contain, and didn't I have my own to tend to?

"It was over twenty fucking years ago," I said. As if grief has an expiration date. I often hoped it did.

It was the worst thing I could have said, but she barely reacted. It was like she'd expected it, like we were both reciting a script now.

"I'm going on a walk," she said.

"I'm coming with you," I said.

"No. Stay in the house."

She walked out, and I threw the dress after her as if it could catch her and hold her in place. But it was so light that it just ribboned slowly in the air before settling on the bed.

I didn't follow Amber. There were only so many times I could chase her.

I DIDN'T KNOW how to pass the time. Calling Amber wasn't an option. There was no service and she hadn't taken her phone. I was too scared to leave the room. I didn't want to run into Pam and Arnold and have to talk to them about our fight or listen to them talk about their dead daughter. I wanted to be in my own home. I wanted to be in my own grief.

I stripped off my clothes and walked the perimeter of the room seven times, but even naked, it was too hot to move. I needed to find Amber. I needed to apologize. We could go home. We could forget all this, go back to the way it was before, when she didn't even talk about her dead sister at all.

I eyed the dress, crumpled on the bed. I had an absurd impulse to put it on, so I did. Why not? I pulled the dress over my head without unbuttoning it. It went on easy, silk-lined and impossibly cold against my body, like I'd plunged into spring water. I rubbed my hands along it. My heart rate slowed. I pulled a little at the fabric of the dress's skirt and watched it shift. It was so delicate. It fit me perfectly. When I looked in the mirror above the dresser, I looked lovely, not the tired, swollen reflection from before. I wanted to kiss myself again.

I TURNED THE KNOB of the bedroom door and peeked out. I didn't see or hear anyone. No newspaper pages flipping, no clanging of kitchen things, no idle chatter, no footsteps. I crept out and down the stairs, went to the front door and slid on a pair of stray blue slippers. I went outside. Sharp gusts rattled the colorful trees. It must have been close to freezing, but I didn't notice. I'd stored up all that warmth from inside. I turned left out of the house and followed a trampled path into the woods, where I assumed Amber had gone to clear her head. Hadn't someone said something about Amber loving the guest house in the woods?

The woods were thick enough to blot out the sun, and as my eyes adjusted slowly to the dark, I saw the house's outline through the starbursts of leaves. It was small, more like a cottage. Many of the surrounding trees would soon stand naked, their leaves lost. But they'd come back. Not dead, just dormant.

"Amber!" I called out, but no one answered other than some noisy birds. Their song a low hum of *churry churry churry churry*.

Twigs snapped under my stolen slippers. The cold still hadn't caught up to me. As I got closer to the guest house, something caught my eye, a light amid the trees. Maybe Amber was there. The light seemed to pull me as I neared. A slipper caught on a felled branch and I left it behind, kicking off the other. Twigs snapped beneath my bare feet, but I couldn't feel them. I felt light, pulled, like I was moving through water.

There weren't just lights on in the guest house. There were candles. Lit candles, one in each window. A real-life version of the dollhouse. It was the same pale blue color. Hardly a manor and hardly nineteenth century architecture, but there was no mistaking the similarities. Helen House, the dollhouse, one and the same. The door yawned open, and the lights blinked at me, and I followed them in.

Inside, the temperature plunged. I hadn't felt it before, but it hit me all at once and I shivered. Thin ice spiderwebbed the windows. Frigid. The furniture looked like the pieces in the dollhouse, magnified to life size. The candles were real, which meant someone had lit them. Someone who had been expecting company.

On a glass table in the middle of the front room sat a doll, hair neatly combed away from her face. I picked it up. She wore a cream-colored lace dress with blue pearl buttons. My hand tightened around the doll's center. I looked up and caught my reflection in one of the windows. Me and this doll in our matching outfits, like warped reflections of each other. My teeth began to chatter.

"Perfect," I heard from behind me.

I turned. A shadowy figure occupied the doorway. "Amber?" I said, dropping the doll.

The shadow stepped in. It was Pam.

"It's what she wants," she said.

"Who?" I asked, though I knew.

"Not just her. All of us."

"I have to go," I said. I tried to move toward the door but I couldn't, my muscles tight from the cold, which suddenly felt unbearable, like I was frozen in place. And yet the body can bear so many things, things that shouldn't be bearable at all.

"I think you should stay," she said. "I've got water on for tea. Warm you right up."

Pam approached and placed a hand on my shoulder. I felt her warmth through the sleeve of my dress.

"Amber will wonder where I am," I said.

"She knows where you are."

My bones felt like an iced-over windowpane, clear glass gone hazy.

When Amber entered, she looked calm, detached. Her hair was pulled back from her face, her mouth parted but she didn't say anything.

"It's fine," Pam said. "I told you it would be fine."

I wasn't sure which one of us she was talking to, but Amber nodded.

"Doesn't she look pretty?" Pam said, and Amber nodded again, slowly, her eyes scanning me.

I wanted to say: *Why?*

I wanted to say: *Let's leave this place.*

I wanted to say: *Did I ever really know you?*

But then, did she ever really know me?

I felt a scratch in my throat, and when I opened my mouth, nothing came out.

I reached for Amber, hoping she would pull me out of this, willing her to be the escape hatch I'd shaped her into. But my arm felt like lead and dropped back to my side.

She has her doll now, I heard someone say. Pam or Amber, I wasn't sure.

Something whistled. A kettle. Tea. Pam left and returned with a regular black kettle, steam swirling from it. She picked up the doll and placed it in a chair at the end of the table, smoothed her synthetic hair with her palm. There was a tea set on the table, not normal sized like the kettle. A tea set for a doll. Pam filled the cups with splashes of hot water. I was so cold I wished she'd just pour it over my head, scald me back to life. My eyes moved to Amber. I knew she needed something from me, something I'd never be able to give.

But I could try.

Don't you understand why I tried?

ABOUT THE AUTHOR / ARTIST

Kayla Kumari Upadhyaya is a lesbian writer of short fiction, essays, and pop culture criticism living in Florida. She is the managing editor of Autostraddle and the assistant managing editor of TriQuarterly. Her work appears in *McSweeney's Quarterly Concern*, *Catapult*, *The Offing*, *The Rumpus*, *Joyland*, *Vice*, *Vulture*, and others. She was a 2021 nonfiction fellow for Lambda Literary's Writers Retreat for Emerging LGBTQ Voices. *Helen House* is her first book.

Kira Gondeck-Silvia is a multidisciplinary artist interested in contemporary forms of hysteria, specifically the ways mental illness complicates communication and creates dysfunction in human connections. She uses animals as a surrogate for corporeal bodies and terror related to gendered power. Her work serves to open up the conversation about the human embodiment of identity—through trauma, privilege, power, and manipulation—exploring how our identities are even formed. She currently lives in Sanford, Florida with her writer husband, four cats she puts bandannas on, and a neurotic dog.

ACKNOWLEDGMENTS

Thank you to Ryan Rivas and Burrow Press for coming to me at the exact right time. I was just about to shelve this project—too long to be a short story, too short to be a novel—when Ryan presented the perfect home for *Helen House*. Ryan always saw what I was trying to do ("ghost story but make it sexy and gay") and helped me get there. To Kira Gondeck-Silvia for the hot and haunting illustrations. To the Dyke Mountain Annual Writing Residency (a fake residency invented by my girlfriend and me) for being the place where I started writing this story, and to the Sundress Academy for the Arts' *real* residency for being the place where I hit send on the final edits. To the writers and editors I have been so lucky to learn from and work with in the past couple years: Saeed Jones, Nana Kwame Adjei-Brenyah, Dantiel W. Moniz, T Kira Māhealani Madden, Patrick Cottrell, Tajja Isen, Rebecca Rubenstein. To the writers I text the most about writing, Drew Gregory and Kelsey Norris, for making art that inspires me. To Emily for the big red blanket and knowing who I was before I did. To Aly, Caroline, Emma, Quiniva, Erin, and Mariah for always feeling nearby even when they're far. To Paul and Mel for taking me in and letting me stay too long. To Jillian for also taking me in. To Becca for always being down for an adventure (and costume change). To Anjali and Alex for being the first people I ever made up stories for and with. To my parents for always supporting my work (even when I don't let them read it). And an ocean of thanks to Kristen, my favorite writer, my love, for her warm heart, playful Sagittarius energy, genius writer brain, and endless encouragement. Every day, she makes me believe in my writing and in the power of queer stories. From this little book's inception to its completion, she was always there, my Florida sunbeam. I'm lucky.

Printed in the USA
CPSIA information can be obtained
at www.ICGtesting.com
LVHW052148090524
779589LV00020B/583